W9-CHV-810

The Toll-Bridge Troll

Patricia Rae Wolff

ILLUSTRATED BY

Kimberly Bulcken Root

Voyager Books
Harcourt, Inc.
San Diego   New York   London

Requests for permission to make copies of any part of the work
should be mailed to the following address: Permissions Department,
Harcourt, Inc., 6277 Sea Harbor Drive, Orlando, Florida 32887-6777.

First Voyager Books edition 2000
Voyager Books is a registered trademark of Harcourt, Inc.

The Library of Congress has cataloged the hardcover edition as follows:
Wolff, Patricia Rae.
The toll-bridge troll/written by Patricia Rae Wolff;
illustrated by Kimberly Bulcken Root.
p. cm.
Summary: A troll tries to prevent Trigg from crossing the bridge on
the way to school only to be outwitted by the boy's riddles.
[1. Trolls—Fiction.   2. Schools—Fiction.]   I. Root, Kimberly Bulcken, ill.
II. Title.
PZ7.W82126To   1995
[E]—dc20   93-32298

ISBN 0-15-202105-1 pb

C E G I K J H F D B

Printed in Singapore

The illustrations in this book were done in pen-and-ink and
watercolor on D'Arches 140-pound hot-press watercolor paper.
The text type was set in Berling by Central Graphics,
San Diego, California.
Title hand-lettering by Judythe Sieck
Color separations by Bright Arts, Ltd., Singapore
Printed and bound by Tien Wah Press, Singapore
Production supervision by Warren Wallerstein and Ginger Boyer
Designed by Lydia D'moch

For Jack, of course.

—P. R. W.

To Marian and Herbert Otthofer
for their kindness and prayers.

—K. B. R.

Today was the first day of school, and Trigg didn't want to be late.

He gobbled his breakfast, grabbed his books, and gave his mother a good-bye kiss.

"Have a good day," she said, "and be careful of the troll."

"Yes, Mother," said Trigg.

Trigg walked across the field, up the big hill, and down the long road. When he came to the little bridge, he stopped and looked around.

Just as Trigg stepped onto the rickety wooden bridge, a terrible, ugly troll jumped up from beneath it.

"This is MY bridge!" the troll snarled.

"But I have to cross the bridge to go to school," Trigg said.

"Why?" the troll asked.

"So I can get smart."

"That's not a good reason," the troll said.

"I have to go to school because my mother said so," Trigg said.

"Oh," said the troll. "THAT'S a good reason."

Trigg started across the bridge.

"Wait!" the troll said, jumping in front of Trigg. "This is MY toll bridge. You have to pay a penny to go across."

Trigg thought for a minute. He couldn't pay a penny every day to go to school. He would just have to trick the troll.

"I have an idea," Trigg said. "We'll ask a riddle. If you answer the riddle, I won't cross your bridge. But if I answer the riddle, I get to cross for free today."

"Oh, goody!" the troll said, jumping up and down. "I like riddles."

"Here's the riddle," Trigg said. "Why does a giraffe have such a long neck?"

The toll-bridge troll hunched down into a thinking crouch. He crunched his face into a thinking frown. *Think. Think. Think. Think.* After a long time, the troll asked, "What's a giraffe?"

"A giraffe is an animal with a long neck," Trigg said.

"Oh." The troll hunched back into his thinking crouch. *Think. Think. Think.*

"I give up," the troll said finally. "Why does a giraffe have such a long neck?"

"Because his head is so far away from his body," Trigg said. "I win! I get to cross for free today!"

The toll-bridge troll stamped his feet. He shook his fists and made awful, angry troll noises. But he let Trigg cross the bridge.

That worked well, Trigg thought. *I'll need many more tricky ideas if I'm going to cross the bridge every day without paying.*

After school, the toll-bridge troll was waiting for Trigg.

"My mother  lives under this bridge, too," the troll told Trigg. "She heard your riddle, and she said you tricked me. She said *I* was supposed to ask the riddle."

Trigg just smiled and quickly crossed the bridge. As he ran for home, he stumbled over a hole in the road.

That gave him  an idea.

The next day, Trigg's mother kissed him good-bye. "Have a good day and be careful of the troll," she said.

"Yes, Mother," said Trigg.

He walked across the field, up the big hill, and down the long road to the bridge. As Trigg stepped onto the bridge, the troll jumped out, looking more terrible than ever.

"This is MY bridge!" the troll snarled.

Not again, Trigg thought. "But I have to cross the bridge to go to school," Trigg said.

"Why?"

"So I can get smart."

"That's not a good reason."

"I have to go to school because my mother said so," Trigg said.

"Oh," said the troll. "THAT'S a good reason."

Trigg started across the bridge.

"Wait!" the toll-bridge troll said, and again jumped in front of Trigg. "This is MY toll bridge. You have to pay a penny to go across."

Trigg pretended to look for money in his pocket. "I don't have a penny," Trigg said. "But I have an idea. Let's ask another riddle. If I answer it, I cross your bridge for free."

OK," said the troll, "but today *I* ask the riddle." He hunched into a thinking crouch. He crunched his face into a thinking frown. *Think. Think. Think. Think.*

After a long time, the troll said, "I don't know any riddles."

"I know one you can use," Trigg said. He whispered it into the troll's ear.

"Oh, that's a good one! How much dirt can you take out of a hole three feet wide and three feet deep?" the troll asked.

Trigg pretended to think. "That's a hard one," he said.

"I win! I win!" the troll shouted. He jumped up and down.

"No, wait!" Trigg said. "Now I remember. The answer is none. There is no dirt in a hole."

The troll stamped his feet. He shook his fists and made awful, angry troll noises.

I hope I don't run out of riddles, Trigg thought as he ran across the bridge.

After school, the troll was waiting for Trigg.

"My mother said you tricked me again," the troll said. "She said you knew the answer when you told me the riddle to use."

Could be," Trigg said, quickly crossing the bridge. As he ran for home, he spied two coins lying in the dirt on the road ahead.

That gave him  an idea.

The next day, Trigg's mother kissed him good-bye, told him to have a good day, and warned him to watch out for the troll.

"Yes, Mother," Trigg said.

Trigg could see the troll waiting for him, looking more ugly than ever.

"This is MY bridge!" the troll snarled.

Trigg took a deep breath. "But-I-have-to-cross-the-bridge-to-go-to-school-to-get-smart-because-my-mother-said-so," he said.

"Oh, that's right. Now I remember."

Trigg started across the bridge.

"Wait!" the troll said. "This is MY toll bridge. You have to pay a penny to go across."

Trigg sighed. "I have another ☀ idea."

"No more riddles," the troll said. "My mother's mad at me because of your riddles."

No riddles," Trigg said. He reached into his pocket. "I have six cents," he told the toll-bridge troll. "If you can guess what kinds of coins they are, I'll give them all to you. I'll even tell you how many coins I have to make the six cents."

"It's a deal! My mother's going to be proud of me this time," the troll said. "I'm good at money."

"I have two coins," Trigg said, "and one of them isn't a nickel."

"You have six cents with only two coins, and one of them isn't a nickel," the troll repeated.

"Right."

The toll-bridge troll hunched into his thinking crouch. He crunched his face into his thinking frown. *Think. Think. Think. Think.*

"I give up," the troll said after a long while.

Trigg opened his hand. There was one nickel and one penny.

"But you said one of them wasn't a nickel," the troll said.

"Right," said Trigg. He picked up the penny and held it up. "This one isn't a nickel." Trigg ran across the bridge.

After school, the troll was waiting for Trigg.

"My mother said you tricked me again," the troll said.

Trigg just smiled.

Yஇou know what else my mother said?"

"What?" asked Trigg.

"She said tomorrow I have to go to school with you. So I can get smart."

Walk to school each day with a terrible, ugly troll? Oh well, Trigg thought with a sigh, *at least I won't have to pay the toll!*

Meet the Author

Patricia Rae Wolff

I've spent tens of thousands of hours of my life curled up reading. I wonder what else I could have done with all those hours. Surely nothing so wonderful as letting my imagination bubble up into words of my favorite stories.

Even television couldn't compete with the pictures I imagined as I read. In my imagination, I was part of the stories. I became the princess in the fairy tales. I rode horses, had a dog, visited far-off places--but only in the books I read. I read funny books, exciting books, all kinds of books--except scary books. I didn't like to be scared. I still don't like horror stories.

As a child, I never thought about the "other side" of the story--the writer's part in the words I read. I never once thought "I'm going to be a writer when I grow up."

When my children went to school, I started to think about the writer on the other side of the book. How wonderful it must be to have a story turn out exactly the way I wanted it. How proud to know other people would be reading it. How exciting to see my words and my name in print.

I started writing. Those thousands of hours of reading and imagining other people's stories became the foundation for writing my own stories.

I wrote first for adult magazines. The most exciting day of my life was the day *Good Housekeeping* called to say they wanted my article for their magazine. And actually paid me for it! I then sold articles to *McCall's, Working Mother* and other magazines.

Later, I spent a short time as Senior Editor for a regional golf magazine, combining three of my favorite activities-reading, writing, and golf. As editor, I got to know the middle, the part between the writer and the reader.

Then one day as I curled up with my granddaughter to read her a book, I remembered that wonder I felt as a child. The wonder of being part of the story I read. I finally knew what I wanted to be when I grew up. I wanted to be a children's writer. I had moved full-circle--back into the world of children's books.

I discovered writing for children is very different from writing for adults. More of a responsibility. Much harder, I think. But also more fun and much more satisfying. I'm only sorry it took me so long to realize I could be a children's writer.

As author of THE TOLL-BRIDGE TROLL, I often have the opportunity to visit schools for Author Presentation and Career Days. I tell the children about the other side of the books they read. In my children's workshops, I help them to see the story from both the writer's and the reader's perspective. And I get them started writing for publication NOW!

Maybe some of them will see how much fun it is to be a writer and say, like me, "I want to be a writer when I grow up." Hopefully, they'll be much younger than I was when they do.

Patricia Rae Wolff

Meet the Troll

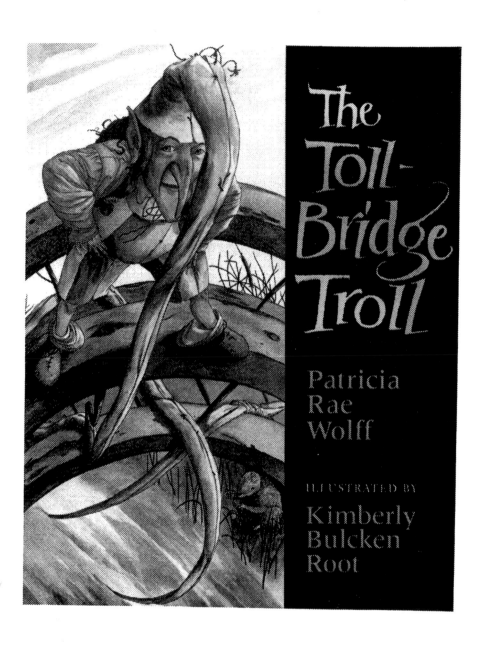

Hartcourt Brace, 1995

- ⭐ An ALA Notable Children's Book
- ⭐ An IRA/CBC Children's Choice for 1996
- ⭐ Storytelling World Award-1996 Winner